felicity Wishes®

Sparkles Café

Spectacular Skies

and other stories

D0318826

A division of Hodder Headline Limited

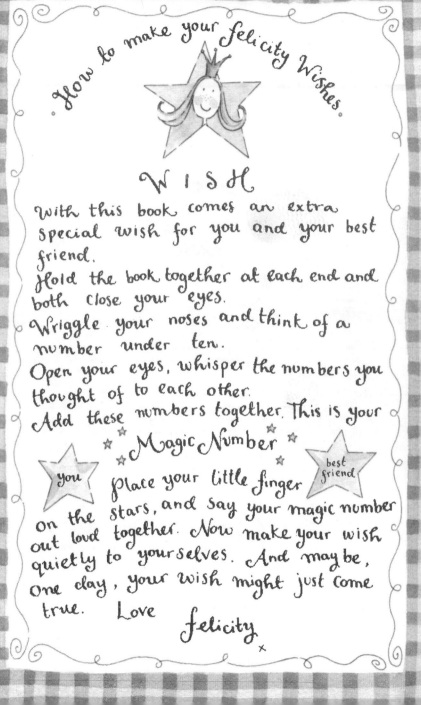

How to make your felicity Wishes.

WISH

With this book comes an extra special wish for you and your best friend.

Hold the book together at each end and both close your eyes.

Wriggle your noses and think of a number under ten.

Open your eyes, whisper the numbers you thought of to each other.

Add these numbers together. This is your

☆ Magic Number ☆

you

best friend

Place your little finger on the stars, and say your magic number out loud together. Now make your wish quietly to yourselves. And maybe, one day, your wish might just come true. Love

felicity

x

For Edie Lingwood
with love and wishes, Auntie Emma x

FELICITY WISHES
Felicity Wishes © 2000 Emma Thomson
Licensed by White Lion Publishing

Text and Illustrations © 2006 Emma Thomson

First published in Great Britain in 2006 by Hodder Children's Books

The right of Emma Thomson to be identified as the author and illustrator of this work has
been asserted by her in accordance with the Copyright, Designs and Patents Act 1988.

A Catalogue record for this book is available from the British Library

ISBN 0 340 91194 8

Printed and bound in Great Britain by Bookmarque Ltd, Croydon, Surrey

The paper and board used in this paperback by Hodder Children's Books are natural recyclable
products made from wood grown in sustainable forests. The manufacturing processes
conform to the environmental regulations of the country of origin.

Hodder Children's Books
A division of Hodder Headline Ltd, 338 Euston Road, London NW1 3BH

CONTENTS

Weird Weather

Felicity Wishes was meeting her friends Holly, Polly and Daisy on the corner of Star Street so that they could fly to school together. But by the time she arrived, a thick fog had descended on Little Blossoming. The high street, the fields, the apple orchard and even the ice rink were all engulfed in fog.

None of the fairy friends could see anything further than the end of their wands. Trying not to bump into each other was proving impossible, let alone trying to fly to school.

"Sorry," said Felicity.

"No, I'm sorry," giggled Polly.

"Oops, sorry!" squealed Daisy.

"Argghhhhhhhh, sorry!" shouted Holly. "I can't see a thing!"

"I suggest we go very, very slowly," said Polly sensibly. "If we all fly straight up and then turn at exactly the same moment, we shouldn't crash into each other again."

"We're going to lose each other, I know it!" squealed Daisy with a mixture of excitement and fear.

"Not if we hold on to each other's wands," said Felicity, thinking on her toes.

* * *

So the four fairy friends began their slow journey to school, Felicity leading them.

"How do you know if we're going the right way?" shouted Holly from the back.

"I can hear the ducks on the pond!" shouted Felicity. "It sounds like they're just under us now."

"And I can smell croissants cooking at Sticky Bun!" called out Daisy. "So the school gates should be coming up any time…"

Suddenly there was an enormous crash and the four fairy friends ended up in a heap on the ground.

"Sorry!" said Felicity, fumbling around for her wand. "It seems the gates are shut!"

The fairy friends' day went from bad to worse. Feeling a little battered and bruised, they carefully walked up to the school entrance... and soon realized that it wasn't just outdoors that everywhere was covered in fog, but inside too!

"This is impossible! Surely they'll cancel today's classes?" said Polly, looking around at the fog-filled assembly hall.

"I don't see how we can have lessons when we can't even read our books or see what we are writing!" said Daisy.

But Fairy Godmother had different plans! She was too busy to take assembly that day so she'd sent Miss Shearing, the deputy head, to tell the fairies that classes would continue as normal.

But lessons that morning were anything but normal!

"I'm going to pass you the ball, on

the count of three," said Felicity to Polly in their netball lesson. "One… two… three." But as Felicity went to throw the ball, something prevented her arms from moving.

"Where did it go?" squealed Polly, darting frantically around in the fog, trying to feel for the ball.

"I haven't thrown it yet!" giggled Felicity, suddenly realizing why she couldn't throw. "I've got my games shirt on back to front!"

* * *

Lunchtime wasn't much better. The four fairy friends had arranged to meet, as normal, under the Large Oak Tree – but by the time they found each other, lunch was almost over!

"I don't know how we're going to be able to watch a film in geography this afternoon," mused Daisy, who'd been looking forward to the treat.

"None of us could see the projector in English this morning."

"There probably wasn't even a projector there!" said Holly. "Actually, that's a point. How does anyone know whether anything's there or not when the fog makes it impossible to see?" she continued thoughtfully.

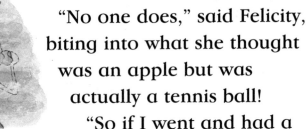

"No one does," said Felicity, biting into what she thought was an apple but was actually a tennis ball!

"So if I went and had a quick haircut now, no one would ever know?" said Holly, her mind whirling.

Holly had just received a last-minute invitation to the *Fairy Girl* Awards and she wanted to look her best in front of all the fairy photographers. Hair Today was normally booked up weeks in advance but Holly was sure that during school time she could get an appointment straight away.

"No, I suppose not," said Felicity.
"As long as you were back in time for
double maths this afternoon."

"But you would need to tell Fairy
Godmother if you were leaving the
school grounds at lunchtime," said
Polly.

There was no answer.

"Holly? Holly?" called Polly into the
fog.

But Holly was long gone.

Daisy had been right. In geography
the film show looked nothing more

than a hazy blur in the distance and the class was left to imagine the exotic places in Fairy World that had been captured on screen.

But next door in double maths, Felicity's thoughts weren't in exotic places. Holly still wasn't back from the hairdresser's and Felicity was frantic with worry that her empty seat would be discovered.

"Now, Holly," said Miss Logic, addressing the fog-covered desk.

There was a long silence. What was Felicity going to do?

"Yes, miss," replied Felicity in her best husky voice.

"Not you, Felicity," said Miss Logic. "I said Holly."

Felicity's eyes opened wide in disbelief. She'd thought her impression of Holly had been spot on. But then she realized that Holly's desk was four rows away from her own. In order to answer as Holly she'd have to crawl under the desks to get to the right seat.

"So, Holly," said Miss Logic, beginning again.

Felicity shuffled across the floor at top speed.

"What answer do you have for question 56a?" Miss Logic continued.

Felicity stopped dead. She'd left her answer sheet on her desk and she was still one place short of reaching Holly's chair. She'd have to wing it.

"Holly?" demanded Miss Logic.

Felicity got to where she thought the desk was and without losing a moment she squeezed herself under the table legs and on to the seat.

"What? What in the Fairy World? What are you doing, Felicity Wishes?" said Miss Logic as she looked down at the shocked fairy on her lap. "And where is Holly?"

"Sorry, miss!" spluttered Felicity, who was more shocked than Miss Logic.

"Wrong desk!"

And the whole class erupted in a mountain of laughter.

* * *

No one knew how they'd made it home that evening. They were just glad they had.

As Felicity landed on her foggy porch she was aware that there was someone standing close by.

"Hello," she said tentatively into the mist.

Slowly something came towards her, sniffing as it moved.

"Hello," said Felicity again, more nervously this time.

The fog made everything eerie. Even the rustle of her plants in their pots was enough to make her heart beat faster.

"I said, hello!" said Felicity loudly, panicking now.

The sinister sniffing shape was almost upon her.

"Oh, Felicity," cried the shape. "It's all gone wrong!"

When Felicity put out her hands to

feel who it was in front of her she couldn't immediately tell. The sniffing fairy was now crying so uncontrollably that there was no way she'd be able to rely on the voice.

"Polly?" said Felicity, feeling the fairy's bobbed hair.

The fairy wailed more loudly than before.

"Not Polly then!" said Felicity to herself. "Look, why don't you come inside where there's a bit less fog and I can see who you are and if I can help."

Felicity opened her door, turned on her hallway light and guided the crying fairy inside.

"Holly!" said Felicity. "I didn't recognize you!"

"My hair!" Holly blubbed. "It's ruined!"

* * *

After pouring them both a strawberry

milkshake (Felicity had poured more on the floor than in the glasses), Felicity and Holly snuggled down on the settee for a chat.

"The hairdressers just couldn't see what they were doing!" burst out Holly. "I was the only customer and Angela, who usually cuts my hair, started to chop, but when she went to answer the phone Phoebe started all over again, cutting the same bit. And when Phoebe realized what she'd done and went to get Angela, a third fairy called Alice, who I thought was

Angela, began chopping some more!"

"So now you have a bob like Polly," said Felicity, getting to the point. "I think it suits you. And, anyway, it will grow again, you'll see. And when it does it will be healthier and stronger than ever."

"Someone has to do something about this fog," said Holly, feeling a little better and wiping her nose.

"I've tried," said Felicity. "I went to see Floella and the other Weather Fairies before I came home. They're just as mystified as the rest of us. Each of them has tried everything in their power to disperse the fog but nothing works. Floella seems to think that the magic that has been used to create this has nothing to do with the weather at all."

"Not the weather?" said Holly, forgetting her hair for the first time that afternoon. "Then what?"

"I don't know. The only person we could think of that could generate that amount of magic is Fairy Godmother, and I'm certain she wouldn't wish such a terrible fog on any of us."

* * *

The next day was just as bad as the previous one. When Felicity opened her bedroom curtains the fog was still there, denser than ever.

When Felicity and her fairy friends finally reached the School of Nine Wishes, the fun that had filled yesterday's classrooms had turned to frustration.

"Don't!" said Polly firmly to the fog beside her. Every time Polly put pen to paper, a mysterious little nudge would pop out of the fog from nowhere and ruin what she was writing. "It's not funny any more."

Holly humphed. Jogging Polly's arm as she wrote had caused all the fairy friends to double up with laughter yesterday. But today the only fairy that found it funny was Holly.

✳ ✳ ✳

"I've got to collect a new timetable from reception," said Felicity at break-time. "You three have fun without me. I'll see you in sewing class later."

"Watch where you go!" called out Polly, concerned for Felicity – who was renowned for being a little clumsy!

"I'll go slowly!" called Felicity, narrowly missing a wall.

✳ ✳ ✳

When Felicity got there, the door to the reception office was open and, by the sound of things, all the secretaries were on a break too.

"Hello?" said Felicity quietly. "Is anyone there?"

"Felicity!" said a startled Fairy Godmother. "Just the person. Can you fly up to that top shelf and reach that large, leather-bound book for me? I've got my finger on a page and if I take it away I'll never find it again!"

Felicity felt the walls around her. She wasn't in reception after all, but in Fairy Godmother's office, next door.

"Yes, certainly, Fairy Godmother," said Felicity, fluttering up slowly.

"You know, for the past two days I've been stuck on a most important question that I simply must answer," said Fairy Godmother. "If you mix rainbow glitter with glitter from the water's edge do you get grade three or grade eight sparkledust?"

Felicity really wanted to help Fairy Godmother but she barely knew the

basics of wish-making, let alone advanced techniques. She flew carefully back down the bookshelf and handed over the large tome.

"Hold my place here, while I have a look in this book," said Fairy Godmother into the fog.

Felicity put her finger on the page.

"It's terribly annoying when you can't find the answer to something that you need," continued Fairy Godmother, leafing through the pages. "I ought to know it, but my head is a little foggy."

"A bit like the weather," said Felicity.

"If only this mist would lift from my mind, I'd be able to see the answer clearly," said Fairy Godmother.

Hearing Fairy Godmother's words gave Felicity a flash of inspiration.

"Fairy Godmother," she said tentatively. "Can I ask you a question?"

"Yes, dear," said Fairy Godmother, "but be quick about it because I've just found a new line of enquiry." And she shuffled some papers on top of her desk.

"Can moods influence the atmosphere?" asked Felicity.

"What do you mean?" said Fairy Godmother, hunting through more papers in her pockets.

"Well, you know when there's a whole hall of fairies about to sit an exam you can feel the tension in the air," offered Felicity.

"Oh, yes, or if fairies are angry with each other you can cut the air with a knife. Yes, I see what you mean," said Fairy Godmother.

"That's it," said Felicity. "So do you

think moods can influence the atmosphere?"

"Oh, yes!" said Fairy Godmother, putting down her papers. "Moods are very powerful things. They can affect things that are seen and unseen. That's why when you make a wish it's very important that you do it with a good heart."

Suddenly Felicity wanted to leap in the air and whoop, but she managed to contain her jiggling wings. She knew she was on to something. "So if I help you find the answer to your question, your wishes will become more clear, less *foggy*?"

"Yes," said Fairy Godmother, "if you put it like that. Now, where did I put that large green wish book?"

* * *

Felicity missed her sewing class. In fact, she didn't attend lessons for the rest of that day.

The clearer the answer to Fairy Godmother's question became, the clearer the atmosphere in Little Blossoming became. Bit by bit the fog lifted from the town to reveal a brilliant crisp blue sky.

"Oh, thank you, Felicity," said Fairy Godmother, when they finally answered her question. "I don't know what I would have done without you."

"And I don't know what Little Blossoming would have done," said Felicity to herself as she flew home, seeing everything clearly for the first time in days. "if you hadn't found the answer to your question!"

The power of your feelings

has a magic that can
affect everything

Spectacular Skies

When the sun shines in Little Blossoming, everybody smiles.

Summer had finally arrived, and Felicity Wishes and her three best fairy friends were enjoying every minute.

"Summer is definitely my favourite time of year," announced Felicity, taking a large slurp of her iced lemonade.

"You said that about winter last year – when we were lying on the snow after a snowball fight!" giggled Daisy.

Felicity thought for a moment. "All weather is my favourite!" she beamed. "I love flying kites when it's windy, and toasting marshmallows when it's cold!"

"How about really big clouds?" said Holly, pointing at the sky.

Felicity, Polly and Daisy turned to look up at the enormous clouds that were looming above them.

"Boo!" moaned Felicity as she pulled on her cardigan. "Clouds are great to fly through, but they don't go with iced lemonade!"

"Summer's not just for lemonade!" said Polly sensibly. "It's the school summer fete the day after tomorrow. Let's fly to Daisy's house to see how our plan is coming along."

✳ ✳ ✳

The School of Nine Wishes annual summer fete was always held at the height of summer. Every year Fairy Godmother asked each of the fairies to contribute in some way.

Last year Felicity, Holly, Polly and Daisy had skipped with ribbons around a maypole, dancing complicated steps that everyone watched in awe. Awe, Felicity remembered, that had quickly turned to disbelief and then a slow crescendo of laughter as the fairy friends discovered that they'd tied themselves up in knots and would need assistance to be set free!

"I'm glad we agreed to do something completely different this year," said Felicity, kneeling down to inspect Daisy's strawberry patch.

"Home-made strawberry ice cream!" said Daisy, licking her lips. "Fairy Godmother is going to be very proud of us."

"They don't look quite ripe yet," said Holly, as she peeped under a leaf at the green fruit.

"Two more days of sunshine and they'll be sweet and red," said Daisy knowledgeably. "In the meantime we can get the stall ready."

* * *

The four friends had designed the stall in art class the week before. It had been Holly's idea to have an enormous cardboard ice cream stuck to the front of the counter, with an opening through which they could hand out their wares. The difficult bit would be making the cardboard ice cream large enough that the four fairy friends and a fridge could stand behind it.

"I don't have a big enough room for us to cut this out," said Daisy, one hand on her hip as she looked at the sparkly card they'd decided to use. "Let's do it out here instead," she suggested, glancing up at the sky. "I'd hate for the weather to ruin all our hard work, but that cloud doesn't look as if it's going to rain."

Making a monster ice cream out of cardboard was harder than it sounded. It was hot work and secretly everyone was happy that the sunshine was hidden behind a cloud.

"What do you think?" said Holly and Daisy together.

Felicity and Polly looked up at the stall front their friends were holding out in front of them.

"It's big!" said Felicity, stating the obvious.

"I think our stall will be the most successful," announced Polly. "It makes me want an ice cream just looking at it!"

"You'll have to wait until the fete for that, I'm afraid," giggled Daisy.

"How about making the ice cream at my house tomorrow?" suggested Felicity, who wanted an excuse to lick the bowls. And everyone agreed.

＊ ＊ ＊

When Felicity pulled her curtains back the next morning she wasn't greeted with the usual burst of summer sunshine. Yesterday's large white cloud still hung in the air, with no breeze to send it away.

Just then, Felicity's phone rang. It was Daisy.

"It's a disaster!" said Daisy, panic in her voice.

"What is?" asked Felicity, still half asleep.

"That cloud hid the sunshine all day yesterday and it's still there today!" Daisy cried.

"We don't need sunshine to have

fun!" said Felicity kindly. "Just look at all the fun we had yesterday, and today we're going to make ice cream."

"That's just it!" Daisy burst out. "We can't make ice cream. There's been no sunshine to ripen our strawberries. We can't make strawberry ice cream with unripe strawberries – it would be green!"

Felicity giggled a little at the thought of green strawberry ice cream. But she knew her friend was really worried, so she reflected carefully for a moment.

"I'll go and find Floella the Frost Fairy," she said. "She's the only fully fledged Weather Fairy I know. She'll tell us what to do."

Felicity got dressed in record time. None of her clothes matched, but today that didn't matter. What mattered was that the strawberries should have time to ripen and be turned into ice cream before the fete the next day!

* * *

Felicity arrived at Floella's front door and rang the doorbell. It didn't seem to make a noise.

The second time she rang, "GGGGGrrrrrrrrrrrrr!" came the sound. Felicity was just about to comment to her little blue bird on the strange chime, when she realized that the sound had come from her tummy. She hadn't had any breakfast!

"Floellllllllla!" called Felicity through the letter box. "Helllloooooooo!"

"Hello!" came a voice from behind her. "Can I help?"

Felicity spun round. "I'm looking for Floella. Do you know if she's at home?"

Floella's next-door neighbour shook her head. "She's gone away on some kind of Weather Fairy conference for a week."

Felicity looked desperate. "Do you know when she's due back?"

Floella's neighbour yawned. "Ummmm – I think she said Sunday. Yes, that's it, tomorrow. She's going to be back in time for the school fete, she made sure of it."

Felicity muttered a thank you and, wings drooping, fluttered away. She didn't know what to do. There was no point in going home to get ready for her friends' visit. Without sunshine there would be no strawberry ice - cream making. Felicity looked up again at the cloud. There was only one thing for it.

* * *

The flight up to
the cloud was a long
one. Felicity wasn't
sure exactly what she
was going to do when
she got there, or how she
was going to persuade it
to move, but she did know
she would have to try.

The closer Felicity got to the cloud, the denser the white billows became. Most clouds Felicity had ever rested on or flown through were a little like cotton wool, but this cloud looked more like balloons. "No wonder it's not moving," she thought. "You'd need a gale, not a breeze, to send this lot on its way."

Then suddenly out of the fluffy white clouds there came a voice.

"Hooray! Help at last!"

Felicity frowned and stopped in her tracks. In the whole of Fairy World she'd never heard of clouds that could speak.

"Over here!" came the faint voice again. "We're so glad you came! We thought no one would ever see us all the way up here."

Felicity squinted.

"Floella!" she called out, recognizing the voice. "Where are you?"

"Here!" came a shout from below her.

And Felicity looked down to see four large wicker baskets full of fairies!

"What's going on?" she asked.

"My fellow Weather Fairies and I are on an international conference in these four super-size hot-air balloons," called up Floella to the hovering Felicity. "They're designed to look like clouds, so that we blend in with the sky. But with four balloons travelling together, our ropes tangled up and we all became stuck."

"We've been here for two days!" shouted another fairy. "We tried to untangle the balloons, but the ropes are so twisted that we can't get out of the baskets! And we're supposed to be arriving at Magic Mountain for a storm display this afternoon!"

Carefully Felicity squeezed her way between the big white balloons.

It was true. All the Weather Fairies were well and truly stuck. Felicity was the only one that could save them and send them on their way.

"Sit tight and hold on. I'm going to try and set you free!" called Felicity.

Using all her wing power, she set about untwisting the balloons and their ropes. If only, she thought, she'd had breakfast.

* * *

Two hours and a lot of sparkledust later the four enormous hot-air balloons were free.

Floella the Frost Fairy, Suki the Sunshine Fairy and Rhiannon the Rain Fairy were the first to be released and able to help the struggling Felicity.

"Thank you!" said Floella on behalf of everyone. "Before you came along we'd all pretty much given up on finishing our conference."

"I couldn't have done it without you," said Felicity, blushing.

"Why don't you come with us?" offered Suki, shuffling up to make

room in the basket for one more. "If the idea of a storm display doesn't excite you as much as it does us then there are plenty of other things to see and do."

"Magic Mountain is home to the most exotic food in Fairy World," said Floella – who had noticed Felicity's tummy rumble!

Suddenly Felicity remembered the school fete, the ice cream – and, most importantly, the unripe strawberries.

"I'd love to," she said honestly, licking her lips at the thought of all the exotic food. "But I'm afraid I have a catastrophe of my own to sort out."

"Is there anything we can do?" offered Suki, Rhiannon and Floella all at once.

Felicity thought for a moment.

"I'm afraid it may be too late," she said, and she told them all about their strawberry ice cream plans.

"Well, there is one thing I might be able to do to help," smiled Suki.

* * *

Felicity sang with happiness all the way home. When she got there she found Holly, Polly and Daisy waiting for her on her front porch in the shade, fanning themselves with old copies of *Fairy Girl* magazine.

"Look at the sunshine!" beamed Daisy as she got up to greet her friend.

"It's hotter than hot!" said Holly.

"The cloud's completely gone away!" squealed Polly.

Felicity wiped her brow. "I know. I'd tell you all about it, but right now we've got some strawberry ice cream to make and I'm starving!"

Daisy looked gloomy. "I'm afraid the strawberries aren't ripe."

"But this is super-strength sunshine!" protested Felicity. "Suki the Sunshine Fairy used two different grades of sparkledust to make it happen."

"Super strength or super-dooper strength," said Daisy, "it wouldn't matter. The strawberries are still green and won't be ripe in time for us to make ice cream for tomorrow."

Leading them into her kitchen, Felicity opened her cupboard, took out a sparkle bar and ate it in one go.

"We can't abandon the lovely ice-cream stall we made yesterday," she said, looking in her fridge for something else to eat. "And we can't disappoint Fairy Godmother by doing nothing for the fete."

Felicity looked at the contents of her fridge and tried to imagine putting something else in a cone instead of ice cream.

"Mashed potato may look like ice cream, but it won't taste right!" said Polly, reading her friend's mind.

"Not even with sprinkles?" said
Felicity innocently, who could imagine
eating anything she was so hungry.

"Why don't we just make plain ice
cream," suggested Holly. "It's nowhere
near as good as strawberry flavour,
but since we don't have anything else
to put in the ice cream, it will be
better than nothing."

"Yes," said Polly. "After all, we've

got all the ingredients except for the strawberries, and it would be a shame to waste them."

"And we can add sprinkles!" encouraged Felicity. "It will be great!"

But secretly she wasn't convinced.

* * *

Sunday morning and the day of the fete arrived. Dozens of fairies from the School of Nine Wishes flew around busily getting their stalls ready. There were coconut shies, jam and cake stalls, hoopla stands and flying displays – but there was one stall that stood out as being far more eye-catching than all the rest.

Holly, Polly, Daisy and Felicity all looked up to admire their enormous ice cream stand.

"Very good, fairies," boomed Fairy Godmother across the village green. "You'll be the first stall I visit when the fete opens!"

Felicity gulped, Holly winced and Daisy and Polly looked at each other nervously.

Plain ice cream was never going to taste as good as strawberry, no matter how good your imagination was.

Just then Felicity felt a tap on her shoulder.

"Floella!" cried Felicity, spinning around to see her Frost Fairy friend. "You're back!"

"Yes! And thanks to you we made it to the storm display just in time."

"We brought you a little something back from Magic Mountain to say thank you," said Suki, peeping out from behind Floella.

"A dozen boxes of rare cloudberries!" said the rest of the Weather Fairies in unison.

"When we saw them, we just couldn't resist!" cried Floella.

Felicity had an idea that nearly made her faint with delight. She couldn't wait to share it with her friends.

* * *

There was just time to mix the cloudberries into the plain ice cream before the fete opened and the first customer arrived.

"Delicious!" cooed Fairy Godmother as she took a huge lick. "I couldn't have imagined anything nicer!"

"I always find that food tastes best when you've made it with friends!" said Felicity, giving Holly, Polly and Daisy an enormous hug.

Trust in the
magic of time

everything is always
alright in the end

Stormy Stand-off

It was very, very cold in Little Blossoming – especially considering it was the height of summer! The weather had been behaving strangely all week.

On Monday Felicity had got up, put on her favourite pink summer dress and skipped out of her front door only to be confronted by hailstones!

When she got to school the whole class was talking about it.

"It's f-f-f-freezing!" moaned Holly, her teeth chattering.

"I'm wet through!" shivered Polly.

Felicity took off her coat and undid her thick woolly cardigan. "For once I'm glad that I was late!" she said. "I'd barely closed the front door before the downpour began, so I was able to go back for more clothes."

Everyone had agreed that Felicity was very lucky.

But on Tuesday, when Felicity left for school prepared for wet and cold weather, she was confronted with a blast of hot sunshine so strong it made all the freckles on her nose come out at once!

The fairies' games lesson on Wednesday was yet another weather disaster. No sooner had Miss Skipping handed out the tennis rackets than the sky opened up and it began to snow!

* * *

"We can't go on like this!" said Felicity, arriving at school on Thursday with four big bags.

"What's in those?" asked Polly.

"Winter clothes, summer clothes, spring clothes and autumn clothes!" said Felicity, exasperated. "I refuse to go another day where I'm either too cold, too hot, too wet or too chilly. Flying everywhere with a dozen outfits is the only way!"

Polly giggled. She thought Felicity was going a little over the top... that is, until she saw Holly!

"I can't be expected to change clothes three times a day and not coordinate!" Holly said, heaving in her portable wardrobe!

That night Felicity couldn't sleep. She pulled on her thick pyjamas and snuggled down under her duvet with her furry hot-water bottle – but woke up, only an hour later, in a sweat. After throwing off her bedclothes and flinging open the window to let in the warm summer air, she sat on the edge of the bed and heaved a sigh.

"The answer to this problem," she said determinedly, "is to find out what's changing the weather. And tomorrow," she thought, "I will do just that."

* * *

But Felicity hadn't been the only fairy in Little Blossoming to have the same thought. Reporters for the *Little Blossoming News* had already found out what was causing the fluctuation in weather, and their story filled the entire front page.

WEATHER FAIRIES QUIT!

"It turns out that after attending a week-long international conference

on weather, each of the Weather Fairies discovered what the others did," said Holly, waving the newspaper in the air as she spoke "But that's good, isn't it?" asked Polly, confused.

"You'd have thought so," said Holly. "But when they found out more about their friends' jobs, they were so excited that they wanted to swap and experience different kinds of weather."

"It says here that the Frost Fairy wanted to try being the Sunshine Fairy and the Rain Fairy wished to swap with the Breeze Fairy," said Polly, studying the article.

"That doesn't sound like such a bad thing," suggested Felicity.

"Well, according to this article, the Head Weather Fairy wouldn't let them change jobs," continued Polly. "She was worried that it would cause chaos. So the Weather Fairies have gone on strike!"

"So what's going to happen? What's the weather going to do until the Weather Fairies sort out their differences?" panicked Holly, glancing over at her portable wardrobe.

"Who knows?" said Felicity, who was secretly a little excited about all the gossip the situation had created. "Star TV are going to interview the Weather Fairies for the six o'clock news at Sparkles café tonight!"

Felicity, Holly, Polly and Daisy could barely concentrate on their classes that day. Not because the weather was all over the place, but because they couldn't wait to fly down to Sparkles and watch the live TV interview. Little Blossoming was going to be famous!

* * *

"Testing! Testing!" announced a prim-looking reporter as she tapped her microphone and skipped over dozens of large snaking cables.

Felicity, Holly, Polly and Daisy squeezed their way to the front. Seated on one side of a long table in the centre of the room were four Weather Fairies looking grumpy and nervous. Bright lights shone in their eyes.

"Five – Four – Three – Two – One – You're live!"

"Welcome to Little Blossoming!" said the TV Reporter Fairy, Philomena Petal, to camera. "A sleepy little fairy town just outside of Bloomfield. Sleepy, that is, if any of the residents could get any sleep! Little Blossoming has been subject to the most extreme

weather conditions Fairy World has
known, and here," she said, motioning
with her outstretched arm, "are the
Weather Fairies responsible for it."

The Weather Fairies looked sheepish.

"Floella," said the reporter, walking

over to the table, "I understand you are the spokesperson for the group."

Floella nodded.

"Can you tell us in your own words why you've created such a storm?"

"Making rainbows... with all that

colour... suddenly seemed like much more fun than bringing in the frost!" Floella said passionately. "I've been doing frost-related magic for so long, the thought of creating something new was too hard to resist!"

Philomena nodded. "And you all felt the same way?" she asked the panel.

The Weather Fairies nodded sincerely.

"So what went wrong?" the reporter demanded.

"The Head Weather Fairy wouldn't let us!" piped up Suki the Sunshine Fairy.

"And not one of us can face going back to our old jobs, so we quit!" burst out Bo the Breeze Fairy.

"So there you have it," said Philomena, turning back to camera. "A vacancy exists for four Weather Fairies in Little Blossoming, and needs to be filled at the earliest opportunity. This is Philomena Petal reporting for Star TV six o'clock news."

"Three – Two – One – Close!"

Shocked murmurs circled the café as the four Weather Fairies got up to leave. Outside, the bright tropical sunshine suddenly turned to snow and everyone groaned.

"We have to do something!" said Polly to her friends.

"It's half-term next week," said Felicity. "Why don't we volunteer to stand in until new Weather Fairies can be found?"

"But we don't know the first thing about being Weather Fairies!" said Holly.

"I'm sure Floella and her friends will help us to get going." Felicity knew the Frost Fairy had a kind heart.

"OK!" said Holly, "let's do it! But only if I can be the Sunshine Fairy.

I've had enough of all this summer-
time snow!"

* * *

Felicity and her friends flew off after
the four Weather Fairies. It wasn't
difficult to catch up with them. One
look at their woebegone faces told
Felicity that she had a chance of
getting them to help. She outlined
their plan.

"But, Felicity, we're on strike!" said
Floella.

"That doesn't mean you can't help
us learn to do your jobs!" said Felicity
in her most persuasive voice.

"Just think of all the plants which are struggling because of the strange weather conditions," added Daisy.

"She's right, you know," said Rhiannon the Rain Fairy. "And I'm sure the Head Weather Fairy wouldn't mind... she'd just be so pleased that someone wants to help!"

"Oh – all right then," agreed Floella.

"Great – it'll be fun!" said Felicity happily.

* * *

With their offer of help accepted, Felicity and her three fairy friends set about becoming temporary Weather Fairies in their school break. Each friend was assigned to a different Weather Fairy. Holly would be taught by Suki the Sunshine Fairy, Polly would be taught by Floella the Frost Fairy, Daisy would be taught by Rhiannon the Rain Fairy and Felicity would be taught by Bo the Breeze Fairy.

For two whole days the fairy friends learnt everything they could about the weather they would now be in charge of.

"It's amazing!" said Polly as she flopped down next to her friends on Felicity's sofa. "I never thought there'd be so much to learn."

"You can't be doing much at this time of year!" said Holly, who was hot and bothered. "Summer's not really the right time for frost!"

"You'd be surprised," said Polly. "The mountains are below freezing for most of the year. Floella's an incredible teacher. She knows everything there is to know about frost. She's even been teaching me the names of every single snowflake."

"I didn't know there were different types of snowflakes," said Felicity.

"There are zillions!" replied Polly.

"The thing that's surprised me the

most about being a Weather Fairy is how the weather you create surrounds you no matter where you go," said Felicity, bringing in a tray of drinks for her friends.

"A steaming hot chocolate for you, Polly," she said, handing the  trainee Frost Fairy a mug. "An ice-cold cherryade for you, Holly, to help cool you down, and a nice warm cup of tea for you, Daisy. Here's to tomorrow!" she toasted, raising her own cup of still lemonade. "Our first day of being real Weather Fairies."

* * *

When the next day dawned Felicity knew the weather from now on could only get better. With her best friends in charge it wouldn't be long before everything in Little Blossoming was back to normal. As she opened her curtains, sunshine filled her bedroom.

"Well done, Holly," Felicity said to herself. "Perfect summer weather, and perfect for doing some washing." She looked around her bedroom floor at the mound of dirty dresses.

* * *

Felicity sang as she pegged out her clean clothes later that morning. Despite having to wear her hair tied back in a ponytail, being a Breeze Fairy, was, Felicity decided, a breeze! And there were definitely advantages. Nothing was stopping Felicity from creating a little wind to help her washing dry – it was her job, and everyone would appreciate it.

Felicity carefully picked up her new Weather Fairy breeze wand and swished it about in the way Bo had taught her. Closing her eyes, she tried to imagine the type of breeze she wanted to create and then, with a large flash of sparkledust, the wish was complete.

Felicity dashed outside to see the results.

Leaves rustled in the trees, the flag on the top of the School of Nine Wishes quivered, and the clothes on Felicity's washing line began to billow. The breeze blew gently at first, then gained strength, becoming more forceful by the moment, until Felicity noticed in horror that one of her dresses had been torn from the line and was circling in the clouds above.

At exactly the same time Holly had decided that on her first day as Sunshine Fairy she'd give the fairies of Little Blossoming a day they'd never forget – tropical heat that would turn home into an exotic island holiday.

Holly stood on tiptoe, just the way Suki had shown her, and waved her wand with a large and forceful sweep, showering sparkledust. The impact of the sunshine wish was immediate, and happened just moments before Polly and Daisy met on top of one of Little Blossoming's mountains.

"It's a bit windy!" noticed Daisy, holding on to her crown with all her strength.

"And it's a bit hot!" said Polly, noticing the frost beginning to melt.

"We should do something before it gets out of hand," said Daisy, who'd noticed that the snowflower leaves were becoming singed in the sunshine.

"Quick, let's go and find the Weather Fairies!" said Polly.

* * *

Floella, Suki, Bo and Rhiannon sat outside Sparkles enjoying a drink in the boiling summer sun.

"This is the life!" said Suki half-heartedly. "Although it is a bit hot. I hope Holly isn't overdoing it!"

"Hmmmnnn," agreed Bo quietly.

"I'm missing the rain," sulked Rhiannon.

"I'm missing the cold!" said Floella as she poked one of her ice cubes with a straw.

"I'm sure Felicity, Holly, Polly and Daisy are doing a wonderful job," said Bo, trying to perk them all up.

"After all, they had wonderful teachers!" said Floella, giggling.

"It's just that there's so much to learn and nothing can replace experience," mused Bo. "We were a good team," she sighed, picking up her drink.

Bo didn't have the chance to take a sip before a strong gust of wind took the straw straight out of her mouth. She also didn't have time to voice her dismay before a pink dress came flying around the corner and covered her face!

"What in Fairy World?" was all Floella could say before they were all engulfed in a whirlwind of clothes.

"What's happened to my lovely sun?" squealed Suki.

"What's happened to my beautiful breeze?" cried Bo above the howling wind.

Daisy and Polly came flying towards the café, fighting against the gale. They quickly explained how everything had gone so horribly wrong.

* * *

It took the four Weather Fairies the rest of the day to put right the mess Felicity and Holly had made. When at last everything was back to normal, they flew off to find Felicity and her friends.

"Weather is like everything," said Floella sternly to Felicity, Holly, Polly and Daisy. "No matter what you do, it will always have an effect on everything else."

Felicity bowed her head in shame.

"Each of us has a talent for something that comes from the heart," urged Bo, trying to make the fairies feel better.

"It's just that weather most definitely is not yours," said Suki earnestly.

"I don't understand what we did wrong," said Felicity, who had followed the Weather Wish instructions to the letter.

Floella thought hard before answering.

"Love of something – true love, that is – is sometimes the one magic ingredient that makes everything come together. Suki, Rhiannon, Bo and I love our chosen weather fields with a passion we have for nothing else."

"So... you love being a Frost Fairy so much, you'd never want to do anything else?" Felicity said with a grin.

Floella realized what she was saying.

"Which I guess means that we won't quit after all!" she burst out, beaming.

"We're glad to have you back!" laughed Felicity. "Little Blossoming has the best Weather Fairies in Fairy World!"

And everyone cheered.

finding out what you
love best
in your heart

will show you how to be
happy in your life

Emma Thomson's

felicity Wishes ®

Daisy is obsessed

with winning Little

Blossoming's Best

Village display in

Dreamy Daisy

Dreamy Daisy

Daisy was the dreamiest of all Felicity Wishes' friends. She was also the quietest, which meant that if you didn't know she was daydreaming, you'd think she was a very shy fairy.

Daisy daydreamed about most things. She daydreamed about how it came to be that the grass was green and not blue, why fairies could fly and animals couldn't. But mostly, she daydreamed about anything and everything to do with flowers. Flowers were her absolute passion: from the tiniest seed through to the largest sunflower, Daisy loved them all.

"Does everyone agree?" said Felicity loudly.

Holly, Polly and Winnie whooped with a resounding, "Yesssss!"

"W-w-what?" said Daisy, coming back down to Fairy World with a bump.

Felicity, Holly, Winnie and Polly looked at Daisy, mouths wide open.

"How can you say 'what'?" said Holly, aghast. "We've just spent the last three days talking about nothing else but the School of Nine Wishes' disco."

But Daisy had other things on her mind.

"Daisy, are you up for working out a dance routine to Susie Sparkle's new single for the disco?" repeated Felicity patiently.

Daisy looked clueless.

"This evening at my house?" prompted Felicity.

"Oh no, I can't!" said Daisy, quick as a flash. "I've arranged to meet Miss Briar. We're discussing the floral displays for Little Blossoming's Best Village entry."

Daisy had never been considered qualified enough to help out on the Best Village team before. Being a novice fairy at the School of Nine Wishes meant that she didn't yet have her double wings or, more importantly, a certificate to be a fully qualified Blossom Fairy.

"Why didn't you say anything before?" said Holly, exasperated. "We're a team, and without you our dance routine just won't be the same."

Felicity quickly stepped in. "Don't worry, Daisy," she said kindly. "We'll work something out."

✳ ✳ ✳

Daisy had no problem concentrating in the meeting with Miss Briar that evening. When Daisy thought of flowers it was as if she flowered herself.

"I was thinking," said Daisy tentatively, as she opened her note-book, "of doing something like this!"

Miss Briar took Daisy's outstretched notebook and looked closely at the page.

"It's wonderful!" said Miss Briar. "Truly inspirational."

Daisy blushed a delicate rose pink.

"And you say you've haven't even graduated yet? I can't believe you don't have your double wings!"

Feeling more confident now, Daisy elaborated. "Well, I thought as the prize-giving is going to be held in Little Blossoming, it will be a perfect opportunity to show the judges why they chose us for first prize!"

"You're very confident that we're going to win," said Miss Briar, impressed.

"I know we're going to win, because I know that no one could possibly love flowers as much as I do!" burst out Daisy.

"Well," said Miss Briar, scanning Daisy's plans again. "These drawings look out of this world. But is that because they are out of this world?"

Daisy looked puzzled.

"What I mean is," continued Miss Blair, "are they achievable? We only have a month until the competition."

Daisy turned the page. "I've been looking on the World Wide Wand," she said. "I was waiting to see what you said before I went any further, but I've already found lots of eager flower growers and professional Blossom Fairies from around the world who are interested in helping!"

Miss Briar quickly scanned the list.

"Well, Daisy, it appears as though you've got yourself a job! You will be

in charge of decorating the prize-
giving garden and throwing a
garden party fit for a fairy queen,
to be ready no later than four weeks
from today."

Read the rest of

Emma Thomson's
felicity Wishes®

Dreamy Daisy

to find out whether

her dream garden

comes true.

If you enjoyed this book, why not try
another of these fantastic story collections?

Designer Drama

Star Surprise

Clutter Clean-out

Newspaper Nerves

Enchanted Escape

Whispering Wishes

7 Sensational Secrets

8 Friends Forever

9 Happy Hobbies

10 Party Pickle

11 Wand Wishes

12 Dancing Dreams

13 Spooky Sleepover

14 Fashion Fiasco

15 Pink Paradise

16 Spectacular Skies

17 Dreamy Daisy

18 Perfect Polly

19

20 Holly's Hideaway

21

Winnie's Wonderland

Fairy Fun

Look out for these three special editions

Summer Sunshine

Christmas Calamity

Winter Wishes

Friends of Felicity

My best friend

My best friend is georgie.
She has been my friend for
three years. Georgie is my
best friend because she is funny
nice and good at thinking of games.
She is very imaginative. She
absolutelly loves fairies!

Goodbye

Molly age seven

Celebrate the joys of friendship with Felicity Wishes!

Felicity Wishes is an extra-special 'friendship' fairy – she's spirited, modern, always there for her friends; she's guaranteed to raise your spirits!

Do you have a friend who you'd like to nominate as your 'best friend'?

Do they make you laugh? Are they generous and kind? Why are they your best friend?

Just nominate your best friend and you could see your letter in one of Felicity Wishes' books. Plus the chance to win an exclusive Felicity Wishes prize!

Send in your letter on A4 paper, including your name and age and with a stamped self-addressed envelope to…

Felicity Wishes Friendship Competition
Hodder Children's Books, 338 Euston Road, London NW1 3BH

Australian readers should write to…

Hachette Children's Books
Level 17/207 Kent Street, Sydney, NSW 2000, Australia

New Zealand readers should write to…

Hachette Children's Books
PO Box 100-749 North Shore Mail Centre,
Auckland, New Zealand

Closing date is 30 April 2007

**ALL ENTRIES MUST BE SIGNED BY A PARENT OR GUARDIAN TO BE ELIGIBLE.
ENTRANTS MUST BE UNDER 13 YEARS.**
Winners will be notified by post, and at the latest within 3 months after closing date.
Winners' letters will be published in a future Felicity Wishes book.
The prize will be a Felicity Wishes product we have in stock which we hope you will enjoy.
For full terms and conditions visit www.felicitywishes.net/terms

Exclusive Felicity Wishes Prizes!

From January 2006, there will be a Felicity Wishes fiction book publishing each month (in Australia and New Zealand publishing from April 2006). Each title will display a different sticker on the front cover. Collect all 12 throughout the year, stick them on the reverse of the collectors' card which you'll find in *Dancing Dreams* or on the website, download from **www.felicitywishes.net**

When you have collected all 12 stickers, just send them in to us! In return you'll be entered into a monthly, grand prize draw to receive a very exclusive Felicity Wishes prize*.

Please send in the completed card to the relevant address below and mark it for the attention of...

Felicity Wishes Collectors' Competition
Hodder Children's Books, 338 Euston Road, London NW1 3BH

Australian readers should write to...

Hachette Children's Books
Level 17/207 Kent Street, Sydney, NSW 2000

New Zealand readers should write to...

Hachette Children's Books
PO Box 100-749 North Shore Mail Centre, Auckland

* A draw to pick 50 winners each month will take place from January 2007 – last draw will take place on 30th June 2007.
Prizes will be a Felicity Wishes product which we hope you'll enjoy.
For full terms and conditions visit www.felicitywishes.net/terms

Would you like to be 'A Friend of Felicity'?

Felicity Wishes has her very own website, filled with lots of sparkly fairy fun and information about Felicity Wishes and all her fairy friends.

Just visit:

www.felicitywishes.net

to find out all about Felicity's books, sign up to competitions, quizzes and special offers.

And if you want to show how much you adore and admire your friends, you can even send them a swish Felicity e-card for free. It will truly brighten up their day!

For full terms and conditions visit www.felicitywishes.net/terms